The Adventures of

PHiL AN THROPY

by
Linda Wise McNay, Del Martin and Ailena Parramore

www.OurFundraisingSearch.com

Published by Fitting Words; Hendersonville, Tennessee. www.fittingwords.net

Authors: Linda Wise McNay, Del Martin, and Ailena Gibby Parramore

Illustrator: Mason McNay

Graphic art services provided by LACreative.

Contact:
Our Fundraising Search
1708 Johnson Rd NE,
Atlanta, GA 30306

linda.mcnay@gmail.com
Phone: 404.895.5942

ISBN: 978-0-9979136-7-5

Printed in China

Our authors are dedicated to bringing philanthropy concepts

to children and their families to help create

more generous and caring communities.

"Phil! Annabelle! Wait up!" yells Thropy, skating to his friends as they headed to the pool.

"How many times do I have to tell you - I'm JUST AN!" steams Annabelle.

Thropy grins—he knew that would get a reaction. "Yeah, whatever. Listen-- I thought we should nail down what we're going to call ourselves. I'm between 'the terrific trio' or 'the triple threat'. Now that we're famous, people are going to have all kinds of questions ..."

"Thropy," Phil sighs. "We've been over this. We don't need a name. We are NOT famous. We're not even out of 3rd grade yet!"

"Well, if what we did doesn't make you famous, what does?" Thropy questions. An pipes up, "statistically speaking, your chance of being famous depends on a number of factors. Your chance of becoming a movie star is one in 1.5 million; becoming President is a whopping 10 million to one. I estimate your chances of becoming famous to be..."

"Alright! Alright!" Thropy exclaims, "Good grief! You seriously have all that in your head? Okay, so we're not famous. But we did change the world a little bit."

Phil's eyes light up, "I have an idea. What if we write down what happened and share it? I'm not sure about changing the world, Thropy, but maybe others would see that you don't have to be an adult or famous to make a difference."

An, smiling in agreement, pulls out a massive notebook from her backpack and says, "Where should we start?"

One steamy day over Spring break, friends Phil, An and Thropy set up a lemonade stand to make a little money.

Phil had been drooling over a waterproof camera for those "once in a lifetime" shots.

An wanted a microscope with an unpronounceable name to add to her impressive home research lab.

And Thropy had his eye on "the sweetest new skateboard" down at the skate shop.

After a couple of hours, a boy about their same age wheeled up with his Dad. "Two fresh-squeezed lemonades coming right up! And by the way, I'm Phil. This is An and that's Thropy. I don't think we've seen you around. Do you live in the neighborhood?"

"Nice to meet you! I'm Ian. And yes, I do live in the neighborhood", replied Ian. The friends thought it strange they had never seen Ian before. They practically lived at the neighborhood pool in the summers.

But there he was.

Ian and his Dad hung out for a while. The friends agreed that Ian was awesome. Not only was he super-smart, but he was also a sports fanatic. "Wow! You know as much about surfing and boarding as Thropy does!" Phil announced as Ian was leaving.

By PHIL

After Ian left, the friends asked Phil's mom why they hadn't met Ian before. "That's unacceptable!" An declared after learning that their neighborhood pool wasn't accessible for Ian. "If one of our neighbors loves to swim, he shouldn't have to be driven to another pool. We should have the lift he needs to get from his wheelchair into the water!"

Disgusted, Thropy chimed in: "You mean to tell me that all these years we could have been playing Marco Polo with Ian, but missed out because there isn't enough money to buy the lift? We have to do something!"

"Yeah, but what? We're just kids," Phil questioned.

And then it hit them. The camera, microscope and skateboard they wanted could wait. This was important!

An, counting the money from the lemonade stand, said, "Okay, today we made $56. Combined with my and Phil's allowances and Thropy's birthday money he hasn't already spent, we have a grand total of $181!"

"We're going to get Ian that chair lift!" the friends cheered.

Unfortunately, it wasn't going to be that easy. After considerable research, An and her mom realized that the type of lift Ian needed would cost $1,500. "At this rate, we'll all be in college before we have enough," whined An.

By PHIL

"We are not giving up that easily!" Phil encouraged. "If we think

this is important, maybe others will, too." So, Phil, An and

Thropy devised a plan to raise the rest of the money: Their

mothers helped them make flyers advertising that they would

work for donations! They emailed the flyer to everyone in the

neighborhood and before they knew it, they were mowing lawns,

raking leaves, and walking dogs.

Phil's next-door neighbor, Mr. Carleton, asked him to help repair the fence around his yard. Mrs. Harper had An help bake dozens of cookies for a party. "How did I get stuck bathing Ms. Harper's cats?!" Thropy moaned. "I'll have scratch marks for the rest of my life!"

that is no thow that happened! those cats were HUUUUGE!!

By PHIL

Then something amazing happened. "You won't believe this!"

An exclaimed running into the clubhouse. "Ella, the girl who

lives next door, just stopped by and gave us money from her

babysitting jobs. She said she heard what we were doing and

thought it was awesome. She'll give us all her babysitting

money until we reach our goal!"

"She's not the only one," Thropy added, "You know Taylor, that

older kid with the sweet backflip off the diving board? He

asked people to donate money to our cause instead of buying

gifts for his birthday. And my sister even donated her tutoring

money (and she's stingy!)"

After just a couple of weeks, all the kids that had helped crammed into Phil, An and Thropy's hideout as An counted all the money collected, "The grand total is...$1,156.43!"

"That's still a l-o-o-o-ng way from the $1,500 we need," Phil said. "$343.57, to be exact. Any ideas?"

After a few seconds, An stood up. "What about a bike rally?" she asked. "We could ask our family and friends to donate money for every lap around the pool we ride." After very little discussion, everyone agreed.

With the help of her parents, An got permission for the bike event, then handed out tasks to her friends.

"I knew she was great at science," Thropy huffed, out of breath from walking the entire neighborhood passing out flyers, "but who knew she was so good at being in charge?"

By PHIL

By the end of the week, An and the friends had marked the route with cones, set up a drink station, made signs to cheer the riders on, and even had music! Now all they needed were kids to join them. And, boy, did they!

The morning of the rally, Ian was sitting at the starting line with a gigantic grin. "Wow! I don't think I've ever seen so many bikes in one place!"

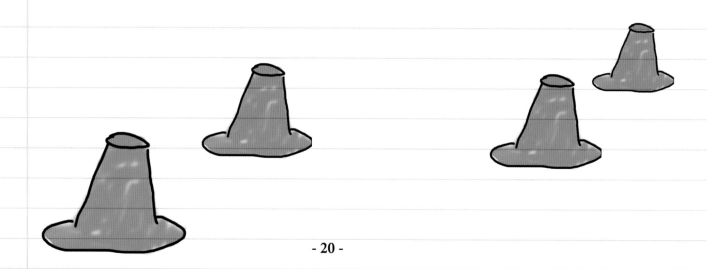

By PHIL

"It was all An's idea," Phil said, tying off the last of the balloons at the starting line. "We just did what she told us to," Thropy grinned, poking An in the ribs.

"It was a team effort," An said smiling. "I may have had the idea, but it took all of us to pull it off."

By: An

With dozens of kids at the starting line, An's Dad announced that he would match dollar for dollar whatever was raised that day. That meant that the total amount of donations raised from the bike rally would be doubled! Amidst cheers he then yelled "Ready, Set, Go!" and they all took off.

A big sign displayed how much they made; after each lap the

crowd cheered louder as the total grew higher and higher.

Neighbors that didn't even know what was going on stopped

by. A few even donated, too.

Everyone was in a great mood,

but no one was happier than Ian.

At the end of the day, they'd done it. Not only did the friends raise the money, but with the match An's Dad gave, they went over their goal by enough to cover the expenses and help with any future repairs.

The lift was installed just in time for the start of

summer break.

And Thropy finally got to play Marco Polo with Ian!

That summer, the kids from the neighborhood kept showing up at the friends' clubhouse, sharing stories about others that could use their help. "We can't stop now," one girl said, "look what we were able to do for Ian!"

"We should form a club!" Thropy exclaimed. "I've been working on some names, but I don't think 'The Terrific Trio' works for a group this large."

Everyone fell silent as An stood up and cleared her throat, "There's only one name that makes sense: The PhilAnThropy Club. We will do what we can, with what we have, to help others."

After a unanimous vote, An was declared the club's President.

She wasted no time plotting their next adventure in Philanthropy.

By: An

Sitting on the sidewalk, An closes her notebook.

"It's perfect," Phil declares.

"You really think people will read our story?" An asks.

"They'll read it. And maybe it will inspire them to start their own PhilAnThropy Club," Phil responds confidently.

"You know, I always wanted to do something important, but I'm just a kid. Well, now I know that I can make a huge impact when combined with others."

"So, we aren't famous," Thropy pipes in, "And maybe we didn't change the whole world. But we did change Ian's world - and that's pretty cool, too!"

How to Start a PhilAnThropy Club

You too can change someone's world by simply following the PhilAnThropy Club's motto: We will do what we can, with what we have, to help others. It may not make you famous, but it will certainly change someone's world!

Step #1: Ask a parent or other adult to help you get started.

Step #2: Who - Which friends will be part of your PhilAnThropy Club?
Who will lead the meetings and keep everyone on track?

Step #3: When & Where - Decide where and when you will meet.

Step #4: What & Why - What do you want to accomplish and why?
Research and compile a list of options.
- Is there a neighbor or family friend that has a need?
- Is there a nonprofit organization that could use volunteers or funds?
- Is there a community organization that has a need you can help meet?
- As a group, do you only want to focus on one kind of need, or many?

Step #5: How - With the help of an adult, discuss all your options and choose which need you
will focus on. Decide what your goal is and then what steps to take to accomplish it.

Step #6: Execute your plan.

Step #7: Celebrate! Once you've met your goal,
celebrate your accomplishments as a team.

Step #8: Decide on your next PhilAnThropy adventure.

We'd love to hear about your PhilAnThropy adventures.
Share your story and pictures with us at:
Linda.McNay@gmail.com